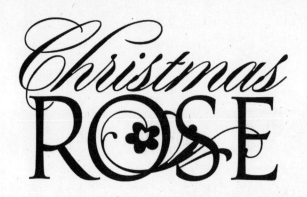

A Novel by

ROBYN BUTTARS

SHADOW
MOUNTAIN

Visit us at ShadowMountain.com

Library of Congress Cataloging-in-Publication Data

Buttars, Robyn.
   Christmas Rose / Robyn Buttars.
   p. cm.
   ISBN 978-1-59038-988-1 (pbk.)
1. Girls—Fiction.   2. Mothers and daughters—Fiction.
3. Cooks—Fiction.   4. Congregate housing—Fiction.   5. Christmas stories.
I. Title.
   PS3602.U8923C48 2008
   813'.6—dc22   2008013024

Printed in the United States of America
R. R. Donnelley and Sons, Crawfordsville, IN

10   9   8   7   6   5   4   3   2   1

*Dedicated to all who recognize and appreciate the power
of unconditional love,
and in memory of my dear parents,
June and Blake Butterfield*

Contents

Acknowledgments

I express my sincere appreciation to Chris Schoebinger for understanding *Christmas Rose* and encouraging my final re-write; Lisa Mangum for her persistence in getting my manuscript read and editing it; Vicki Parry for her valuable editing; Richard Erickson and Sheryl Dickert Smith for the beautiful cover and design; and Tonya Facemyer and Rachael Ward for excellent typesetting work.

I gratefully acknowledge my proofreaders, Sarah Buttars, Chalese Buttars, and Crystal Burningham.

Chapter One

HOME

Pleasant Manor stood among the surrounding corn-
fields like an oasis in the desert. Freshly painted
white siding glistened in the sun except on the sides
where golden tassels of ripened cornstalks stroked at the
walls with each wisp of wind.

"This is my stop." Rosie's words were barely loud
enough for the driver to hear.

"Here?" The bus driver turned in his seat to look at
Rosie.

She knew his next question before he asked it. Each
time a new bus driver took her home the same thing
happened.

"You live at Pleasant Manor?"

Rosie was looking down at the floor, letting her
thick, brown ponytail cover her face. "Behind it." She

1

stepped past the driver and waited on the bottom step for the automatic door to slide open.

"Do I pick you up here tomorrow?"

"Yes." Rosie's voice blew in the breeze as the door shut behind her. She stood for a moment, needing the calming peace of her quiet country home after her first day of fourth grade.

Corn and grain fields stretched in every direction. The distant city, which she could barely see, seemed like another world—a world she had to put up with each day, but a place in which she could never feel at home.

New bus drivers were always surprised when they dropped Rosie off in front of the care center, as if a child could not belong in such a place. However, Pleasant Manor was where Rosie felt at home. It was like Bessie said: "Home is a place where you are surrounded by love."

The heavy wooden door creaked on its ungreased hinges when Rosie pulled it open far enough to slip through. As she walked down the hall and into the great room, the smell of hot, sticky, cinnamon rolls made her stomach churn with anticipation. Her eyes darted around the room, jumping past each empty chair until she spotted the tip of a gray bun of hair, barely showing over the top of Bessie's old wing-backed sofa.

Rosie slipped quietly behind the sofa and placed her hands around Bessie's eyes. "Guess who?" Her voice was deep as she tried to fool her friend.

"Well, it couldn't be Harry or Lily or my little Rosie. No, indeed, it couldn't be my little Rosie or she would have given me a big hug." Bessie's delight with the game was obvious as she pulled Rosie's arms away from her face and around her neck in a grandmotherly squeeze.

Rosie clung to her longer than usual, drawing pleasure from the scent of her lilac perfume. Bessie's large, fleshy arms cuddled her in the warmth of love.

"Now tell me about your first day of school." Bessie slid to the corner of the sofa and patted the seat beside her so Rosie could sit down.

"It was all right. My teacher's nice but—"

"Help me! Get the dog!" Helen's cry streaked across the great room as she stumbled through the doorway, pushing her walker in front of her. "The dog—it's in my room!"

"Can you help her, Rosie?" Bessie's gentle push on her elbow moved Rosie to her feet.

She walked toward Helen as Bessie called, "Helen, don't you worry. Rosie will come and help you with that dog."

Helen had already turned around and was walking as fast as her swollen legs would allow. "That dog shouldn't be in my room—"

"Helen, don't worry. I'll take care of it." Rosie had to take giant steps to keep up with her. It was always a surprise to see how quickly Helen could move when she was upset. Any other time her steps were slow and seemingly painful.

Rosie wanted to get to the room before Helen so she could have a quick look around. If Helen got there first, Rosie would be in for a good ten-minute check of every corner and shelf before Helen would calm down.

She ran into the room, looked under the bed, in the bathroom, and in the closet. Then she ran and met Helen at the door. "Helen, the dog's gone. It won't hurt you."

Helen looked at her for a minute, questioning her words, and then, as suddenly as the incident began, it was over. Her look of fear changed to one of haunting emptiness. Helen walked off down the tiled hallway.

"Rosie, you're late today," Mama said as Rosie came into the kitchen. She looked up from the tray of rolls she was frosting. Her words were not a rebuke, just a question.

"I was helping Helen with the dog."

"Oh." The simple word held understanding. "How was school?"

Rosie pulled a chair next to the counter and took the cinnamon roll that Mama placed on a napkin for her. "Okay, I guess. We had a new bus driver and he didn't want to let me off here."

Mama laughed. Her long dark ponytail that was so much like her daughter's swung back and forth as her body shook with the sound. "Adults stay away from care centers until they have to come to one."

She picked up the tray of rolls, set it on the service cart along with a spatula, then opened the door of the oversized oven and pulled out a large tray of meat.

"Mmm, that smells good."

"It's your favorite. You'd better go to the house and

get your homework done so you can be back in time for supper."

"It's the first day of school, Mama. There's no homework."

"Do you want to help me?" Mama handed Rosie a tray of salt and pepper shakers before she could respond.

Rosie didn't have to be told what to do. Her routine tasks had been a part of her life as long as she could remember. Each meal, each day, Rosie carried things from the kitchen to the dining room tables, saving her mother a few steps. "You're my legs, Rosie," Mama often said as she sent Rosie on a task.

It wasn't that Mama didn't have legs; it was just that they were crippled, deformed from the hips down. A visitor to the Manor had once commented that Mama's walk looked like a waddling duck in pain. In the kitchen, where everything was close at hand, she moved quickly, but walking any distance took her twice as long as anyone else.

As Rosie straightened the napkins and placed the salt and pepper shakers on each table, she thought back to the first time she had helped her mother at Pleasant

Manor. In her mind's eye she could see herself reaching up to place a roll on the table next to Bessie. But she was never really sure what she actually remembered. The tale of that first experience had been repeated so often, and by so many people, that she could not separate their memories from her own.

Rosie was two-and-a-half years old when they moved into the three-room stone farmhouse behind the care center. Mama was just nineteen.

Although the job as an assistant to the cook was supposed to be temporary, it offered more security than Mama had known since her husband had walked out. For over a year, she had faced the fight to provide for two with the stoic determination she had mastered as a child. To live had always been about survival, not ease or happiness.

Since there was nobody to watch over Rosie, Mama received permission to keep her in a playpen in the kitchen. All had gone well for the first few months—until Rosie decided to have an adventure.

Some parts of that day were clear in her mind. One thing she remembered was the feel of cold metal in a chamber that was quiet except for the hushed echoes that played on the sides. Rosie had climbed out of the playpen when Mama stepped into the dining room with a water pitcher. When Mama returned, Rosie was not there. She had been told what happened—after eight years, the tale still lived!

The cry went out that Rosie was missing. Everyone forgot about dinner as the residents combed the Manor looking for the toddler. People who had not moved by themselves for years pushed their wheelchairs along the halls as they called out for Rosie. It was not clear how long the search lasted. The time it took to find her ranged from fifteen minutes to an hour and fifteen minutes, depending on who was telling the story. But when Rosie toddled out of the huge metal mixing bowl where she had fallen asleep, their shared joy was unreserved. Nobody knows how the bowl got on its side, but it was the perfect size for a toddler to curl up in when she could not find her mother.

At that moment Rosie had become everyone's special friend. "Please send Rosie out with a roll," a resident would request, wanting a chance to get a hug from the toddler.

Mama quickly realized that Rosie would never stay

in the playpen once she had tasted freedom. Her only hope was to keep Rosie busy while she completed her shift. Rosie thought it was a great game, going from table to table for hugs or tastes of her favorite dessert. When Mama took over as chief cook, Rosie became chief runner.

She grew up day by day, year by year, eating, playing, and living at Pleasant Manor. It was only in the evening, when the kitchen was clean, that she and Mama stepped out the back door and walked to the small house. That is where they slept—in the house—but when Rosie thought of home, she thought of the big building next door, the place where she was surrounded by love.

Chapter Two
BESSIE

Pleasant Manor was built years before Rosie was born. Mr. Blackburn, the owner of the little stone house and the acres of farmland that surrounded it, donated a piece of land for the care center. People said that he wanted his wife to be taken care of in her old age. He planned the spot well, close enough that he could visit without having to leave his farm.

When the care center was finished, everyone in the small community expected the neighboring city to expand to the west to include them, but that growth never happened. Pleasant Manor had remained a lone building amid the fields. Mrs. Blackburn died long before her husband did, so he lived alone in the little house, never visiting the large building next door. It was after his death that Rosie and her mother found their way to Pleasant Manor.

The little stone farmhouse was due to be torn down when Mama got the job in the kitchen. But she and Rosie were alone and needed a place to stay. Those in charge decided to leave the farmhouse as it was until other arrangements could be made—arrangements that never happened. Whenever talk of tearing down the farmhouse arose, a cry went up from the care center residents and their families. They wanted Mama to stay, to cook the pot roasts and vegetables, turkey and stuffing, and pork chops and rice in their favorite way. Mama had become a valued employee, but anyone who talked to the residents realized it was little Rosie they could not live without. She had become their sunshine, the center of their attention. She had given them a purpose in life, someone to watch over, to protect, and to love.

Bessie referred to Rosie as her "reason for living." The expression always brought a smile to Rosie's face even though she did not understand what it meant.

To Rosie, Bessie was the life of Pleasant Manor. She had a laugh that flowed from deep within in a sort of sing-song way. It was loud but never seemed out of place. In fact, her laugh made any program a success because it was irresistible—everyone else had to join in.

She loved to talk and would sit for hours visiting with anyone who would listen. Rosie liked to hear Bessie's deep vibrating voice as she shared her memories.

Bessie grew up on a farm a short distance from Pleasant Manor. She was the middle child of eleven so she was never alone. Rosie loved to hear her tell of "working 'til I thought I'd drop." She claimed to have gotten in on the tasks given to the older and younger children.

Rosie would rock with laughter when Bessie told about her first and only time of trying to get out of work. It was very early on a warm summer morning when the six older children went to hoe sugar beets. Bessie was so tired that when her brothers and sisters were busy she curled up on a grassy ditch bank, behind a thicket of bushes, and fell sound asleep. Nobody missed her until it was quitting time. When her older sister found her asleep, she nearly exploded with anger. If Bessie didn't do her fair share all the children would have to work longer to complete the task.

It was getting too hot to finish the job so all the children returned home and told of Bessie's bad behavior. A family council decided, by the vote of the children, that Bessie would have to weed her rows that night with a lantern for light.

Bessie went to the field alone, with only an oil lantern for company. She was not frightened because it was close to her home, and besides, she loved to be out at night where she could see hundreds of stars gleaming against a black sky. She set the lantern in what she thought was a safe spot and began hoeing around the sugar beets. She hadn't gone far when to her surprise the lamp tipped over. She turned just in time to see a skunk lift its tail and spray its legendary scent all over her.

"My girl, I'll tell you that was the last time I ever went to sleep on the job. My mama was up half the night boiling water and scrubbing me with lye soap and ashes to get rid of the smell." Bessie would always stop talking then because her laughter would get in the way. She told Rosie many times, "Something that was downright horrible when it happened can be the most humorous event when remembered."

Rosie often wondered what it would be like to have ten brothers and sisters, or even one. "Did you love having a big family?" She knew the answer before she asked.

"My laws, yes. I was never lonely because there was always somebody to play with or work with. You know, Rosie, you're darn near as lucky as I was. You've always got someone here to be with. Yep, you've got the next best thing to having ten brothers and sisters. You've got yourself twenty people who love you just like your own grandparents would."

It was through Bessie's eyes that Rosie came to understand much about people. Bessie had a keen sense of caring about newcomers to the care center. When a new resident arrived, Bessie was the first one to visit them. Before long, she would have Rosie in her room drawing a picture or making a little welcome gift. As they worked, Bessie would share her insight into the newcomer's life. "My little Rosie, our new resident is in a lot of pain," she would say. "You know there's nothing like a big hug and kiss for getting rid of pain." When they finished the welcome gift, she'd send Rosie to meet the stranger. Rosie's welcome seemed to work miracles. After introducing herself, she gave the agreed-upon hug and gift before hurrying on her way, leaving a new friend behind her.

Mama said life had not always been easy for Bessie.

She came to live at Pleasant Manor right after Mama started working there. Bessie's only daughter brought her to the Manor after a stroke left her temporarily paralyzed on her left side. Bessie had left the only home she'd ever known, her privacy, and all the treasures she had saved in her seventy-seven years. When Bessie's daughter kissed her good-bye, she decided it was her time to die. She never left her room. In fact, she never left her bed if someone didn't make her get up. One of the nurses would have to sit beside her during each meal and force her to eat.

"I guess, in a way, you saved her, Rosie," Mama explained as she repeated the story of Rosie's disappearance. "Bessie was alone in her room that night you disappeared, sitting in her wheelchair. When one of the aides popped their head through Bessie's door, to see if you were there, Bessie followed her out. The next thing we knew Bessie was in the kitchen calling for you. It was strange that she could get that far by herself but I think she is the one who woke you up. Anyway, when I ran back into the kitchen she had you on her lap, hugging you with her good arm."

"How did I get on her lap?"

"Bessie said you climbed up and gave her a kiss because she was crying. You weren't that friendly back then, but I guess it must be the truth."

"I'm happy she found me." Rosie could not imagine life without Bessie.

"After that, Bessie acted like a different person. She wanted to live. She'd get out of bed each day and practice walking with her walker. Before long she was watching over you every time I turned around." Mama would always smile when she remembered.

Chapter Three

CLESTON

Cleston was one of the first people Rosie welcomed to Pleasant Manor. He was a large white-headed man who, when she first met him, looked like a phantom from a horror movie. His dull, expressionless eyes were sunken into his thin, drawn face. Since his dentures were in a cup by the bed, his jaw drew upward so his gums could rest together. That gave his face a very wrinkled texture, much like a piece of old leather.

Bessie tried her hardest to prepare Rosie to meet their new resident. "Cleston doesn't look well. He has pneumonia so he has a hard time breathing. I'll wait right here for you," she promised as she opened the door and scooted Rosie inside with the card they had made for the newcomer.

Hesitantly, Rosie approached the bed where the

man was lying. She was so small that she could see only the side of his body that was not covered by a blanket. Then she heard a noise that made her stop in her tracks. If it were not for her love of Bessie, she would have run the other way. The noise—a gurgling, straining, gasping sound—was coming from the bed. Rosie didn't dare move.

The next thing she knew Bessie was by her side. "Cleston, this is Rosie. She came to welcome you."

He sat up and began to cough—deep, violent coughs that shook his whole body. Rosie hid behind Bessie's leg, scared by the noise of something she didn't understand.

Finally the cough stopped and Cleston seemed to see the little girl for the first time. He wiped his eyes to clear away the tears that came with his coughing, and then reached out a hand to touch the mass of dark curls on her head. "So this is Princess Rosie." His lips tipped up in a half-smile. As he drew in his breath, Rosie heard the noise that had frightened her. It was the noise of his breathing.

She handed him the card, then slipped back to

where she could keep an eye on the newcomer. "Are you Bessie's granddaughter?"

Bessie began to laugh. "Are you, Rosie?"

Rosie just stared at the man but did not speak.

"No and yes. She's not my granddaughter by birth, just by choice, my choice." Bessie pulled Rosie close in a big hug.

"Hmm, I'd like a granddaughter like that." Cleston stood up and opened the drawer by his bed. Then he held out to Rosie a package of Smarties.

"Thank you." Her little fingers reached out into his open hand as she took the package.

"Rosie, do you think you could be my friend?"

Rosie nodded, then waved good-bye and ran out the door.

In the weeks that followed, she learned that Cleston's room was full of treasures. There was always something new waiting for her to see or touch or eat when she popped in to say hello. Because she was too young to read, she had no way of knowing that he had put her name on his candy jar after that first visit. It was never empty. As he came to know her better, he kept it stocked with her favorites.

Sometimes when she visited he would show her the wooden bears or cowboys he had carved. She loved to touch their smooth surface and stare into their life-like faces.

When he got well enough to work in the craft shop, he cut out blocks and animals for her. Cleston's gifts were the only toys she could remember playing with. He was never too busy to help her stack the blocks into corrals, and he taught her how to pretend to be a farmer with the wooden animals.

"Rosie, have you ever seen where milk comes from?"

"From the 'frigerator." Rosie thought the answer was right until Cleston began laughing.

"Rosie, my girl, I'm here to tell you the 'frigerator doesn't make milk. No, indeed—cows make milk."

Rosie's eyes and mouth opened wide in surprise. "Cows?"

Just then the nurse came by, wheeling her supply cart to each resident who needed her care. Cleston got a plastic glove from the box on the cart and filled it with water, and then he poked a hole in the tip of each finger.

"Look here, Rosie. This is like a cow. Milk comes

out just like this." He squeezed the fingers of the glove to force a trickle of water out of each fingertip.

For Rosie it was a new game, squeezing the glove and seeing the steady stream of water, but she still could not imagine how such a thing happened with a cow. As he answered her questions Cleston could see that understanding would not come just with words.

"I wonder if you'd like to visit my farm and see how a cow works," Cleston thought aloud.

Rosie looked up, her eyes pondering the thought.

"Well, would you like to?" he invited her.

"Yes! Yes!" Rosie squealed with excitement and she began to dance around, unable to contain her pleasure.

"I'll see if that can be arranged." Rosie walked beside Cleston's wheelchair as far as the kitchen door, and then she ran inside to tell her mother.

Some memories of childhood are so unique that, though dimmed by time, they remain fresh and vibrant in one's mind. Such was the case with Rosie's visit to the farm. It was during a warm, fall morning that Cleston's son drove Cleston, Rosie, and Rosie's mother there in his pickup.

The first thing Rosie saw when the truck door

opened was a row of little white houses. Inside each house was a black and white calf. "Look at the calves," Rosie's mother said, and she took Rosie's hand and walked slowly toward the hutches.

"Baby cows?" Rosie leaned against the wire that enclosed the houses and stared, eye to eye, at the babies.

"Do you want to pet them, Rosie?" Cleston showed her how to put her hand through the small holes of the wire fence and stroke the calf's head.

As Rosie reached inside the pen, trying to touch the calf, it turned and licked her hand with its long, coarse tongue. "Oh, it got me!" Rosie cried out in surprise.

Cleston smiled. "That just means it likes you," he said as she backed away from the pen. "We'd better get to the barn before they finish milking." He led the way toward a red building.

Once inside the barn, Rosie could smell the cows and hear a clanging sound, followed by a loud swish. Huge cows stood on a platform surrounding her. For a moment she was frightened because they were so big. Cleston sensed her fear.

"They won't hurt you, Rosie. No, sir. They're fine animals. Look here." He pointed to something that looked like the glove he had filled with water.

Rosie's mouth dropped open in surprise when she saw milk coming out of the tips of the udder and running through a clear pipe into another room.

Cleston laughed and for the first time in weeks Rosie heard that strange, strained sound that had frightened her when she first met him. Cleston sat down and lifted Rosie to his lap. Together they watched as the hired man washed the cow's udder then slipped on a milking machine. Cleston's breathing grew quieter until it was completely lost in the surrounding noise.

"Where does milk come from?" Cleston whispered in Rosie's ear.

"Milk comes from cows!" Rosie clapped her hands in delight. She understood.

"Dad, did you want to show Rosie the pony?" Cleston's son stepped up next to his father's chair and held out his arm to help Cleston stand.

"Pony?" Rosie was off Cleston's lap in a second, ready to run out the door.

Her mother hobbled along, trying to catch up with

Rosie before she got to the animal. Just outside the barn, a young boy stood holding the reins of a brown miniature pony.

"Curt, you've taken good care of that pony," Cleston said, placing his hand on his grandson's shoulder.

Curt's pleasure at the compliment was evident in his smile. "May I lead Rosie around on her, Grandpa?"

"She's your pony. That would be mighty nice of you."

He turned to his little friend. "How about it, Rosie? Do you want to ride?"

Without a moment's hesitation, Rosie nodded, her face lit with excitement. Cleston lifted her into the saddle while Curt explained how to hold on. Then Curt began to lead his pony as it bore Rosie like a medieval princess. She waved to her mother and blew a kiss to Cleston.

Ah, the memory—the unforgettable memory of swaying back and forth on the back of a strong, gentle beast. There was the smell of fresh hay and corn silage—things Rosie couldn't put a name to yet, but the day was all so clear in her mind. It was a snapshot in time.

It wasn't long after their farm visit that Cleston and Rosie started taking walks outside. He made birdcalls that sounded just like the real ones. Rosie laughed as birds answered him.

With each walk, with each birdcall, Cleston grew stronger. His breathing was no longer loud and raspy, and he never used the wheelchair.

One day when Rosie went into the craft shop she saw a wooden rocking horse painted exactly like Curt's pony. Cleston was hammering nails into the rockers. His back was toward the door, but somehow he knew she was there. "Come over here, Rosie girl, and ride your horse."

In one quick movement he lifted Rosie, put her on the seat, and set the horse to rocking back and forth. He watched her, a smile of satisfaction curling his lips. "What will you name him?"

"Cleston." It sounded like a whisper above the squeaking motion of the horse.

From that day on, the horse went from the little house to Pleasant Manor every day. Rosie couldn't bear to let it out of her sight. She dragged it up and down the hall as she made her rounds among friends. Always, as she passed Cleston's empty room, she thought of him and the gift he had given her before he left Pleasant Manor. He would not be forgotten by the little brown-haired girl—there would always be two Clestons that she had loved.

Chapter Four

CHRISTMAS SURPRISE

The winter holiday season at Pleasant Manor was the busiest time of the year. Relatives and friends arrived to wish the residents a merry Christmas and happy new year. They seemed to enjoy the strings of cranberries and popcorn that lined the halls, and the green boughs with twinkling lights that adorned the windows and counters. Always on the first day of December a tall, fragrant pine tree was placed in the corner of the great room. Large red, shiny balls were scattered on its branches, along with white lights and red bows. It marked the beginning of the festive holiday season.

The tree had always been Rosie's favorite decoration, but the year that she entered kindergarten it changed from something to look at to something full of magic. That year, before the Thanksgiving holiday, children in Rosie's school class began talking about Santa Claus. Rosie was amused at their stories. She had never heard of such a person and found their tales to be full of the most exciting dreams. She mulled the stories over and over in her mind until she had to know why Santa Claus had never visited her.

"Mama." Rosie was sitting on the stool in the kitchen, watching as her mother iced a tray of sugar cookies. "Mama, does Santa Claus visit old people?"

Mama's eyes jumped from the frosting to Rosie's face. They had never talked about Santa. "I don't suppose so, Rosie."

"Do you think he doesn't know I'm a little girl?"

"What do you mean?"

"Jill said Santa Claus visits all boys and girls on Christmas. He's never come to me. Maybe he thinks I'm old."

"Because you live here, at Pleasant Manor?" Mama put down the frosting and walked over to sit beside Rosie.

Rosie nodded. "Do you think that's why he never comes?" Rosie thought she had found the reason.

"Oh, no, Rosie . . ." Mama reached over and

hugged her little girl. Several minutes passed, then Rosie felt her mother tremble. When she looked up she saw that her mama's eyes were wet with tears that spilled onto her cheeks.

"Mama, I'm sorry." Rosie's voice trembled with emotion. Mama seldom cried.

"It's not your fault, dear. Oh, Rosie, I wish you could have a Christmas like the other children in your class. Maybe someday Santa Claus can visit you, just like he visits them." Mama's eyes lifted from Rosie's face to the kitchen door.

"Am I interrupting something?" Bessie had opened the door just far enough to look inside.

"Come in—we were just talking about Santa Claus." Mama turned back to her work.

"Ahhh . . . Santa. That jolly old man." Bessie's eyes lit up like the Christmas tree in the great room.

"Do you know Santa?" Rosie asked without surprise.

"Well, in a way I do."

"Oh, what is he like?" There was wonder in Rosie's voice.

"Haven't you ever heard of Santa?" Bessie touched

Rosie's long braid as she looked beyond her face into Mama's eyes.

"Santa has never visited me."

"Hmm. Tell me—if Santa came this year what would you like him to bring you?"

Rosie's lips curled up and her eyebrows curved down as she thought. "A baby doll that drinks from a bottle."

"That sounds like a pretty good wish to me. Now that you know about Santa Claus, I wouldn't be surprised to see your wish come true."

"You think Santa Claus will come?" Rosie jumped off the stool and into Bessie's arms.

"I wouldn't be surprised," Bessie said, and she laughed with Rosie over their shared secret. "Right now there's a Bingo game starting. Do you want to play?"

"Run along and have a good time," Mama said as she opened the door for Rosie and Bessie.

That year the holidays took on a special flavor of excitement. Rosie felt the thrill of a secret hope, the hope that Santa Claus would come. When visitors came and sang Christmas carols through the hall, Rosie would tag along behind them. Each time they sang a song that she knew, she joined in with all her heart. Words and music seemed to blend into a promise of tomorrow. Always before the visitors left they shared candy or homemade cookies with Rosie.

"I wish I had something for you," Rosie said to a little girl who was visiting with her parents.

"Oh, no!" The little girl shook her head. "We just want to give to you."

Two weeks before Christmas, Rosie and Mama arrived early at the Manor to prepare breakfast. Much to their surprise, they found a large box full of Christmas candy on the counter where Rosie sat to watch her mama cook.

"What is this for? I didn't order any candy." Mama picked up the note that was folded on top of the candy and read: "To Rosie, Merry Christmas."

"This is yours." Mama shook her head in surprise. "What will you do with all that candy?"

Rosie touched the chocolate bells, the peppermint candy canes, and the chocolate marshmallow trees. In front of her was more candy than she had ever had. "I'm going to share it. I can give it for Christmas presents."

From then on, each visitor to the Manor received a

piece of her Christmas present. Bit by bit, the box of candy dwindled, marking off the days until Christmas. On Christmas Eve Rosie scooped up the last pieces of candy to share with her dearest friends, the residents of Pleasant Manor.

Mama cooked turkey and dressing with cranberry sauce and pumpkin pie for their Christmas Eve celebration. As the residents feasted on the special meal, Rosie walked from table to table with her gift. A big hug accompanied each piece of candy.

While Mama cleaned up the dishes, Rosie wandered into the great room to be by herself with the beautifully trimmed tree. White twinkling lights cast shadows like playful animals around the room. She watched their funny patterns as she moved very near to the tree. Then she realized something was different. Scattered around the base of the tree were wrapped packages. Rosie had never seen presents under the tree at Pleasant Manor. She knelt down beside them and traced the Christmas patterns on the wrapping paper with her finger. There were big and small packages sporting bows and tinsel. They reminded her of the presents her classmates talked about.

"Rosie, it's time to go home," Mama called from the hall.

Rosie jumped up from the floor and ran to her mother. "Mama, there are presents under the tree."

"Presents? Maybe somebody left them there for the residents. They can open them tomorrow."

"May I watch?" Rosie nearly danced with excitement.

"Sure. We'll go in after breakfast. That's probably when they'll open them."

That night Rosie dreamed of Santa Claus coming to Pleasant Manor and leaving a baby doll in a cradle under the tree. He was a jolly old man who sang as he worked. Just before he left, he turned and winked at Rosie. She ran to the doll and carefully lifted the treasure into her arms. Santa had come.

The dream seemed so real that when Rosie woke on Christmas morning, she was sure there was a baby doll waiting for her in the great room, under the Christmas tree. She dressed quickly and ran alongside Mama through the soft snow that had fallen in the night.

"Mama, please come and see the tree."

"But I have to get breakfast ready. We can after that."

"Please, Mama." Rosie pulled on Mama's hand as they walked past the kitchen.

When Mama turned on the great room lights, Rosie glanced around, expecting to see the doll. But nothing had changed from the night before.

Rosie felt a stab of pain in her chest. For a month she had hoped for Santa, expecting that he would come. And the dream . . . what about the dream? She pressed her eyelids together to keep the tears in place.

"Let's get breakfast," Rosie said. She turned from the tree and walked toward her mother. She had hoped, she had dreamed, but Santa had not come.

"What is it, Rosie?" Mama took hold of Rosie's arm before she could leave the great room. Then she sat down on the chair next to the tree so she could look into Rosie's face.

Rosie burst into tears. "Santa didn't come."

"Oh, Rosie, you believed he would." Mama pulled her close. As she reached into her purse for a tissue, she saw the word "Rose" in large, black letters on a nearby package. She picked up the present and smiled as she glanced from gift to gift. "Rosie, my girl, I think Santa did come."

"But he didn't. There's not a baby doll."

Mama held the present in front of Rosie as she read the card: "'To the Rose of Pleasant Manor.' Who do you think that is, Rosie?"

"Is it for me? Did Santa bring it last night?" Rosie pranced around with the present tucked safely in her arms.

"I think so. Let's put it back under the tree. We'll come in here after breakfast."

Rosie was so happy she couldn't stop thinking about the gift under the tree. Even though the residents were in a festive mood, they didn't visit with each other much that morning. One could feel a current of excitement as they ate their breakfast with haste. Mama was cleaning off the last table when Bessie opened the door and said, "Rosie, I think Santa came. Come and see."

Rosie and Mama followed Bessie to the great room. The shadows of the tree lights danced once again, but this time they bounced off the faces of the residents. Each person was smiling and laughing, sharing the happiness of the day.

"Come over here," Bessie beckoned as she led Rosie and her mother through the maze of chairs to the tree. "Merry Christmas, Rosie!" she cried as she placed a large wrapped package in Rosie's arms.

Then one by one each resident left his or her chair and picked up a gift from under the tree. Worn faces were bright with smiles as they placed their packages next to Rosie. "Merry Christmas, Rosie," they said.

Mama sat in her chair smiling and shaking her head in amazement. As she looked at the gifts piled around her daughter, she saw that each contained the same note: "To the Rose of Pleasant Manor. Love, Santa."

Rosie would never forget that Christmas. Santa Claus came. She had more gifts than she would ever have dreamed of—including the most beautiful, perfect baby doll she could have ever wished for. Yet, as she looked back on that day, it was not the brightly wrapped presents or the treasures they held that made her smile. No, indeed, it was the room full of people. Something about them reminded her of the jolly old man with the long white beard. Somehow she knew that she had caught more than a glimpse of Santa Claus.

Chapter Five

HELEN

The next autumn, a few weeks after Rosie started first grade, an unusual cold spell froze the flowers, and turned the field corn to crisp, brown stalks. One's breath seemed to freeze in the chilly air like the icicles that crusted the bushes. Everyone pulled out winter coats and mittens much earlier than was the custom. Even on the bus, Rosie found comfort in the warmth of the knit mittens that covered her hands.

Due to the bad weather, the bus ride home took longer than usual. When the yellow bus finally pulled up in front of Pleasant Manor, Rosie was waiting by the automatic door. As it opened, she could see a woman sitting on the ground. Two nurse's aides from the Manor stood on each side of her.

"What's going on?" The bus driver had been watching the scene since turning at the corner.

If he expected Rosie to answer, he was mistaken. She pretended the words had never been spoken as she jumped from the bus and ran toward the woman, who was wearing only a light dress. The woman leaned forward with her hands covering her face as though she were crying. Before Rosie reached her side, she could hear the aides making threats as they tried unsuccessfully to pull her to her feet.

"Why don't we just leave her here?" one of the aides asked. Laughter followed the question, both of them appearing to think it a big joke.

The woman on the ground paid no attention to them as she rocked back and forth on the icy cement. She was in a world of her own, caged in by a mind that at times comprehended no physical pain.

Rosie fell down on her knees in front of the woman, then took the woman's face between her small gloved hands. "Helen," she said softly. "Helen, please stand up and go home." The words were louder than at first, but still gentle.

There were no tears in Helen's eyes as she looked at Rosie. In fact, there was nothing but a foggy distance, which seemed to clear for one moment to show understanding. In that moment, she stood up and walked toward the door as if that was what she had planned to do all along.

"How did you do that?" One of the aides glanced from Helen to Rosie and back to Helen. Her eyes and mouth were open in a shocked expression.

"Oh, you've never met our Rosie, have you?" the other aide began to explain. "She can get these old people to do something when nobody else can."

Rosie turned from their conversation and ran to open the door for Helen, and then she took off her coat and put it over Helen's shoulders to protect her red, cold arms. Helen did not seem to notice any of these gestures as she went through the door and down the hall. Rosie stayed beside Helen until they reached the nurse's station.

"Helen is really cold," she whispered to the nurse on duty.

As she ran to the kitchen to see her mother, Rosie thought about what the aides had said. It hurt to hear her friends called "old people" in a negative tone. Bessie had taught her long ago that "Some people are old when they are children; others are young even though their bodies have been around for a long time."

Rosie was not sure how Helen fit into that thought. She remembered days when Helen was full of life, a spunky kind of life that kept everyone alert and watchful. Bessie and Helen had been roommates then, and they loved to have fun together. They always included Rosie in their adventures because they could say they were doing it for her—they were helping Rosie to have a good time.

How well Rosie remembered the Fourth of July when they put "Pop-Its" on the door to the shower room. When the morning aide pulled on the door to start the showers running, she dropped to the ground, afraid that somebody was shooting a gun down the hall. Of course they had not meant to cause trouble, and in fact they may have even felt bad about that prank if someone different had been the one to hit the floor. But Rosie had heard Bessie and Helen laugh with pleasure when they found out it had been the aide who shortened their showers to increase her own break time. After all, their showers were something they needed and looked forward to. How could they feel bad when she left them only partially clean and dry?

Then there was the time Helen found Rosie reading alone in the great room. "Rosie, come on. We're going for a little fun."

Rosie was out the door before Helen was. There was no way she would miss a fun event.

Together they went to the storage room. Bessie was waiting inside with three wheelchairs, one of them a child's size.

"We'd better hurry before somebody finds us," Bessie said as she pushed the pediatric wheelchair toward Rosie.

Rosie didn't have to be told what was going on. As soon as the three were lined up, she counted down, "Three, two, one, go!"

Across the room they raced, again and again, keeping track of how many times each one was the winner. The scene must have looked like a clip from *The Three Stooges,* but they didn't care. They raced until Bessie and Helen were exhausted. Rosie was a little scared to ask the aides to push her friends back to their rooms, but she had to. They could never have gotten back on their own.

It took about a week for Bessie and Helen to walk on their own after that. It even took great effort to move from their beds to a chair. "Oh, these old bones," Bessie complained when Rosie visited them. "My insides are a lot younger than my outsides."

"But wasn't that fun?" Helen would never admit to her old age. "I can't wait to do it again."

"I don't think I'd better do that again," Rosie said. "Mama thinks I sprained my ankle." Rosie didn't want to tell her friends that the nurses had begged her to talk the ladies out of such fun in the future.

Bessie and Helen looked at each other, then at Rosie. "We certainly don't want you to get hurt, Rosie dear," Bessie said. "Maybe we will have to do something a little easier for you." Helen nodded in agreement. She could go along with that if she was not the one to call a halt to the fun.

"I know—let's make a Halloween Haunt." Helen's idea seemed like a perfect solution.

With those words, plans were under way to turn Pleasant Manor into a Halloween Haunt. A truckload of pumpkins was delivered to the craft shop, where they were carved into wild, scary jack-o'-lanterns. Ghosts made from sheets and pillowcases, with old clothes as stuffing for the heads, hung eerily in corners and doorways.

It was truly an unforgettable Halloween. The glow from a hundred pumpkins was the only light for the guests. Each person was met at the door by a ghostly phantom who sat the guest in a wheelchair before pushing him or her down the halls. Witches and skeletons slipped out from dark door frames and closets to scare the amazed victims. For someone who was not familiar with the Manor, the halls seemed to stretch forever, hiding one's worst nightmare.

It was a Haunt created just for the excitement of being scared. Since only the families of the residents received invitations, only a small group enjoyed the night, but they would never forget it. In fact, the following spring the Manor began to receive requests for another Halloween Haunt, but it was not to be. Sometime during those months, from Halloween to spring, Helen became a stranger.

Looking back on that time, Rosie vividly remembered

one terrible day. She had run into the room to visit her friends during a winter blizzard and found Bessie standing by the door with tears running down her face.

"I know you took it." Helen's harsh voice echoed along the empty halls.

Rosie saw Helen standing on her bed, surrounded by piles of broken keepsakes and ripped papers. In her hand was the gold-framed picture of her son that she was accusing Bessie of taking.

Rosie walked over to Helen and in a quiet voice said, "Helen, get off the bed."

Helen had never been one to agree to anything without raising a question, but she did just what Rosie asked of her. Bessie went to the bed and cleared a spot for Helen to lie down, then sent Rosie for the nurse.

Rosie didn't see Helen for a couple of days after that. Her doctor put her in the hospital to run tests. When she came back she seemed normal at times, but at other times her words made no sense. She began screaming down the hall about seeing a dog in her room. Her fear was real even though the dog was not. Sometimes she refused to go back in her room for days.

"Rosie, go show Helen there's no dog," Bessie said. She knew that when she tried to help, Helen only responded with anger.

"Come on, Helen." Rosie took Helen's hand and gently pulled her down the hall to her room.

"No!" she screamed. "There's a big dog in my room."

"I'll go in first." Rosie left the door open as she searched the room.

Helen watched her warily from the hall. Fear was etched on her face and evident in her eyes that shifted and searched the quiet room.

"Come in, Helen. There's no dog." Rosie encouraged her from the middle of the room.

Helen didn't move.

"Come on, Helen." Rosie walked over, took Helen's hand and coaxed her into the room. Helen followed.

As time went by, Helen spoke only about things that were not real to Rosie. She seemed to have a different world in her mind, a world that only she could see—one that seemed unhappy and scary.

One day when Helen's family was visiting, Rosie heard her grandson say, "Grandma, do you remember my name?"

Helen looked at him, but did not answer.

When they left, Rosie heard the boy's father explain. "Son, don't be so sad. Your grandma doesn't know any of us."

Rosie couldn't believe that was true. She went in and sat by Helen on her bed. "Helen, what's my name?"

Helen just shook her head and looked away.

"Rosie, she doesn't remember yesterday or even this morning for that matter, but she understands your love." Bessie reached out and folded Rosie in her arms.

Rosie was too young to understand or even question what had happened. Helen had changed, that much Rosie knew. She also understood what Bessie meant about Helen and love.

Rosie was one of the few people who could calm her down. For some reason, Rosie's little voice, and the pull of her hand, got more attention from Helen than the rough threats or tugs of adults.

Helen responded to Rosie's kindness. For Rosie, it was a simple, obvious way to treat someone she loved.

Chapter Six

JAKE

When the pansies beneath the kitchen window peeked out from the spring frost, Rosie began to count the days until summer vacation. Three months of freedom stretched in front of her like a timeless journey of happiness. She loved the opportunity to choose her own activities for the day.

The sidewalks and patio in front of the Manor were an invitation to play hopscotch and jump rope. It was on one such day, as she was skipping along the patio with her rope, that a large black car pulled up to the curb.

Rosie stopped at the edge of the walk and watched from the corner of her eye. A woman in a blue suit got out of the driver's seat, walked around the car, and opened the door.

"Papa, I'm sorry we have to leave." The woman's

voice trembled. "I know you don't want to stay at the Manor. If I could be here and take care of you I would." She reached over the seat and took out a pair of crutches.

"Stop fretting, girl." Although it was a command, there was no sharpness to the man's tone.

"Okay, Papa. It won't be long." The woman stepped to his side and took hold of the man's arm.

From where Rosie stood, she could see a head of white hair rise above the car door. She watched in amazement as the man straightened. His head kept going up, up, up. Rosie's rope fell to her side as she turned to stare at the stranger. Though she knew he was only a man, she couldn't help but wonder if he was as tall as the giant in her book of fairy tales.

It was not until the car door closed, and the man stepped forward on his crutches, that she glanced away from his head. Then she saw a sight that filled her with horror. One of his pant legs dangled loose with no leg to fill it. She stepped back behind the patio chairs, wishing she could run and hide from the fear that grasped her. Yet she couldn't take her eyes off the pant leg that swung to and fro with each forward movement.

Looking neither to the right nor to the left, the man's eyes focused straight ahead to the door of the Manor. It took only a moment for the man and woman to disappear through the squeaky door. Rosie searched the grounds of the Manor, wishing there were someone who could explain about the strangers. No one was there. Rosie was alone.

She opened the door just far enough to slip through, then ran down the hall toward the kitchen. Even though she heard voices behind the office door, Rosie ran past without a glance.

"Mama. Mama!"

Mama hobbled out of the cooler, a look of concern on her face. "What is it?"

"There's a man. He doesn't have a leg."

"Oh . . ." Mama breathed a sigh of relief. "Did he come in here?"

"Yes. Have you seen someone without a leg?"

"Some people are born without legs or lose them in accidents. I guess none of our residents had that problem." She turned away from Rosie to peel the potatoes into the sink.

"Does it hurt?" Rosie wanted to understand. It seemed so strange.

"I suppose so. Was he in a wheelchair?"

"No. He has crutches."

"Can you help me with the tables now?" Mama wasn't trying to change the subject but there was work to be done.

Rosie knew there was nothing left to discuss. She picked up the salt and pepper shakers and headed for the dining room. As she straightened the napkins, she was thinking so hard about the man that she didn't hear the door open until the woman's voice made her jump.

"This is very nice, Papa."

Rosie spun around in surprise. She glanced from the dangling pant leg up to the clear blue eyes of the stranger.

He smiled. "Good morning, young lady."

Her fear vanished. She grinned at the man, somehow knowing she had met a new friend.

He didn't come to lunch, but that night at dinner Rosie found him sitting next to Bessie. He watched her as she walked across the room to give Bessie a hug.

"Is she a friend of yours?" he asked when Rosie looked over at him.

Rosie nodded.

"Have you two met?" Bessie turned to question the man.

"I bet this is the Rose of Pleasant Manor that you've all been talking about." The man put his hand out in front of him.

When Rosie reached out to shake it he said, "Pleased to meet you."

"Pleased to meet you." Rosie's identical reply made him smile.

Although she was not afraid, she was still curious about living with only one leg. As she shook his hand, she found her eyes wandering to the chair where just one full leg reached to the floor alongside the empty pant leg.

"Rosie, this is Jake. He's going to be with us for a while." Bessie's voice pulled her attention away from the stranger. There was something different about her voice, something Rosie couldn't understand.

"Hi, Jake." Rosie looked back into the stranger's face.

"Bessie tells me you're the sunshine in this place. I hope we can be friends. By the way, I can't eat chocolate chip cookies. Can you?"

Rosie nodded her head. "They're my favorite."

After dinner, Rosie waited for Bessie to leave. She needed to talk to her, to ask about the missing leg. Bessie was the one person who would answer her questions until they stopped coming. When she saw Bessie stand to leave she slipped out the kitchen door to meet her in the hall, but found to her surprise that Jake was walking beside her. For the first time, Bessie didn't seem to notice her standing there. She and Jake went by without a glance in her direction.

It wasn't until the following morning that Rosie was able to get Bessie alone. Even then, she seemed to be unusually quiet.

"Bessie, where is Jake's leg?" Rosie finally blurted out, not able to contain the question another minute.

Bessie looked at her for a moment, then closed her eyes and turned away. When she turned back, Rosie saw tears running down her cheeks.

"Rosie, I'm not sure how Jake lost his leg, but it was during World War II when he was a soldier in Germany.

We thought he was dead. The report came that he was missing in action."

"Was he your friend?"

"He was . . . my very special friend. He was gone for three years before the war ended. Then, to everyone's surprise, he came home . . ." Bessie's voice dropped to a whisper. She stepped away from Rosie's side and sat down on a nearby bench.

"How did he lose it?"

"I never heard, Rosie. It was a horrible wound that had begun to heal. I never talked with him alone after his return because I was married by then." Bessie looked out the window, seemingly far away from the little room in Pleasant Manor.

"Good morning, ladies." Jake's voice brought Bessie's head around in a quick movement.

"Jake." Bessie moved over on the bench so there was room for him to sit down.

"And how are you today?" Jake eased himself down to the bench as he looked at Rosie.

"Hi, Jake." Rosie smiled at him and then waved to Bessie before scooting out the door to play.

Several days later Rosie found Jake sitting alone in his

room. When she stopped in front of his door he called out to her.

She walked slowly through his door, somewhat shy though not afraid. He was sitting on the side of his bed and when she entered he pointed toward a nearby chair.

"How old are you, Rosie?"

"Six." She almost held up her fingers before she realized she was too old to do that.

"Do you like it here?"

Rosie nodded her head, then darted a curious glance around his room. It was a plain room. The only furniture besides the bed was a chair and a table with a television on top. One painting hung crookedly on the wall. She was turning back to look at Jake when something in the corner caught her eye. Her head jerked quickly back to verify what she had seen. Then she stiffened with fear when she realized that propped against the wall was a leg.

"Ah, you see my leg." His eyes had followed her glance.

"Your leg?" Her voice trembled.

"You don't need to be afraid. It's just a plastic leg. When I get over my infection I'll wear it again." His voice was soft and soothing.

Before she realized it, Rosie blurted out the question that nobody had been able to answer. "Where's your real leg?"

"Well, now, that's quite a story. Are you sure you want to hear about it?"

Rosie hesitated a minute before nodding her head in answer. Jake looked at her as though wondering if he should explain the circumstances to a child. Then he opened his drawer, pulled out a small plastic case, and handed it to her.

"Do you know what that is?"

In the case was a pin with a ribbon on it. It was different from any pin she had ever seen. She looked back at Jake and shook her head.

"That's a Purple Heart, an award that is presented to wounded soldiers. I received a severe wound to my leg in a terrible battle. It never got better, Rosie, so a German doctor had to take it off."

Rosie's eyes were wide with shock. "He took it off?"

"He had to or I would have died." Jake was trying to explain without frightening Rosie away. "I've been able to live just fine without it."

"Why did people think you were dead?"

Jake looked at her for a moment before he spoke. "How . . . how did you know that?"

"Bessie told me."

Jake turned away from Rosie and sat quietly looking out the window. Somehow Rosie knew he was remembering another place or time. It was something she had grown accustomed to with her Manor friends. Even Bessie did it once, just days before, when she talked about Jake.

Rosie finally cleared her throat, uncomfortable with the silence. Jake turned to her and shook his head. "Sorry. What did you ask me?"

"Why did people think you were dead?"

"I was a prisoner of war for three years. They never let me write home. When I came back people were shocked to see me . . . especially Bessie." His voice had become so quiet that Rosie was not sure she heard it right.

"Bessie?"

Jake reached into his back pocket and pulled out his wallet. After thumbing through the individual compartments, he took out an old picture, wrinkled and torn on the edges. He looked at it before handing it to Rosie.

The picture was of a man and woman standing together in front of a waterfall. She recognized the man. He was very tall and though his hair was black, she could see her new friend in his face. He was standing beside a girl who had long, light-colored hair. Their clothes were different from any she had ever seen.

"Who is this?" Rosie pointed at the girl.

"That's your friend, Bessie, when she was a young lady."

"Why do you have her picture?"

"I took it with me when I went to war. It was my connection to home, to the girl I planned to marry . . ." Jake stopped, shook his head, then cleared his throat and continued quietly. "I had almost forgotten about it. Would you like it?"

Rosie's smile was the answer. "Thanks, Jake," she said as she waved good-bye.

She ran to show the picture to Mama. "Look what Jake gave me!" she called as she opened the kitchen door.

Mama stepped beside her. "That looks like Jake," she said as she looked over Rosie's shoulder at the worn photograph in her daughter's hand. "He was a nice-looking young man, wasn't he? He must have had black hair. Who's the girl?"

"That's Bessie, Mama." Rosie handed her the picture.

"Bessie?" Mama bit her lower lip as she turned the picture toward the light for a closer look. "That's Bessie? Hmm."

She handed the picture back to Rosie and started to fill the sink with water. "Who told you that was Bessie?"

"Jake."

"I guess he knows. You'd better put that in a safe place. That's a treasure, Rosie."

Rosie carefully put the picture in her pocket for safety before leaving the kitchen. Mama didn't need to tell her it was a treasure—she already knew.

Chapter Seven

FRED

J ake stayed only one month at Pleasant Manor. When it was time to leave he walked down the hall without his crutches. One would never guess by looking at him that a prosthesis gave him mobility, but Rosie knew, and she couldn't help but stare. He walked so straight that she was afraid he would hit the door frame as he walked beneath it. In fact, she thought she saw him bend just a little. Once again, he did not look to the left or to the right, and certainly not behind him. He had already said good-bye to the few friends he had made.

Rosie saw him coming out of Bessie's room right before he headed down the hall with his suitcase.

"There you are." Jake reached out his hand to Rosie, just like at first. "It's been a pleasure knowing you, Rosie. You'll look out for Bessie, won't you?"

They clasped hands as Rosie nodded her head. Then Rosie watched him walk down the tiled hall.

When Jake had turned the corner and gone from her view, Rosie ran after him. Residents had come and gone—that was nothing new for her—but none had filled her with such curiosity. Even as he opened the door and disappeared into the warm afternoon, she wondered how he made the leg stay on and how he could possibly walk.

She ran back to Bessie's room and knocked on her door several times before she heard the welcome words, "Come in, Rosie."

"Jake's gone." Rosie felt like crying.

Bessie was sitting in her old rocking chair with a book on her lap. Rosie could see, as she stepped to her side, that it was a picture book. On its pages, faces of people she did not know were frozen in time. Bessie turned the pages, one after another, paying little attention to her visitor until she stopped, her hand on a picture of a woman and man standing in front of a waterfall.

"You were pretty, Bessie." Rosie touched the picture that matched the one hidden in her treasure box.

"I was so young then." Bessie's voice was quiet, barely a whisper, as she shook her head.

"How old was Jake?"

"Jake?" Bessie lifted her head and looked at Rosie. "How did you know it was Jake?"

"He told me."

Bessie put the book on the bed and stood in front of Rosie. She put her hands on Rosie's shoulders and then asked quietly, "Rosie, what do you mean? Did Jake have the picture?"

Rosie had never seen Bessie act so surprised yet so determined. She knew that whatever her friend wanted to know must be very important, yet she was reluctant to answer. Would she say the wrong thing? What did Bessie want to hear?

Rosie just nodded her head in answer to the question.

"Where was the picture?"

"In his wallet. He said it was his connection to home and to the girl he planned to marry . . ." Rosie stopped talking because Bessie was backing away from her.

Without another word, Bessie turned from Rosie

and leaned against the window ledge. Then slowly, methodically, she shook her head as she stared out into the morning sun.

Rosie went to her side and slipped her little hand into her friend's hand. Bessie clasped it tightly. They stood together, yet alone, in their private world of thought.

Bessie seemed different after that. She stayed in her room most of the time. The other residents missed her words of welcome and her quick laugh. Rosie missed her best friend.

"I think Bessie is depressed," Mama said as she tried to help Rosie understand why Bessie had changed.

Within a couple of days, a new man moved into Jake's room. Rosie took her paints and paper to Bessie's room, planning to make a card for the newcomer, but Bessie told her she was too tired to help. Rosie did it alone.

She waited until Fred was watching TV in the great room, then she slipped up beside him and held out her hand, just as she had seen Jake do. "Hi, Fred. I'm Rosie. Welcome to Pleasant Manor."

Fred just looked at her for a minute, then he took

her hand and said, "Well, Rosie, I'm pleased to meet you."

With that done, Rosie turned and ran off down the hall. Fred's pleasant laugh echoed throughout the great room.

Two days later, after breakfast, Fred called out to Rosie as she skipped past his room. Rosie stepped back and looked through the partially open door. Fred opened the door wider and invited her to sit down in his large leather chair.

"Rosie, I've noticed that you seem to know everybody here. Since I'm new I thought you could tell me about them."

"Okay." Rosie was always pleased to talk about her friends.

And so it was that Rosie and Fred began their walk around the Manor. When Rosie told him a person's name, he wrote it in his notebook.

"Why do you do that?" she asked. It was the first time she had seen somebody carry a notebook on a walk.

"Well, I'm almost ninety years old," he began to

explain. "My children want to give me a party and I want them to invite each of the residents."

"A party? May I come?"

"If you're free on August first, you may be my special guest."

"That's my birthday," Rosie said.

"That's my birthday!" Fred laughed. "Maybe we can share it. Would that be all right with you?"

Rosie nodded up and down, making her pigtails jump on her shoulders. It was settled. There would be a party for Fred, with Rosie as the birthday guest of honor. She couldn't wait to tell Bessie.

"Bessie!" She was yelling before she reached Bessie's room. "Oh, Bessie, Fred is having a birthday party. He's going to share it with me."

Bessie's lips turned up into a smile, the smile Rosie loved. Rosie asked, "Will you help me make a card?"

Bessie held out her arms for Rosie. Then she hugged her for the longest time. When she finally let Rosie go, Bessie nodded her head. "You bet. I'll help you."

Bessie took out her best pencils and paper and set them on the table. "Do you know when his birthday is?"

"It's the same as mine!" Rosie was excited to share the news.

"Won't that be a day? Is Fred a nice man?"

"Oh, yes. Come on and meet him." Rosie tugged at Bessie's hand until she followed her out of the room.

By August first, the day of the party, Bessie was smiling and laughing, just as she had always done. When Fred's children carried the birthday cake into the room, she belted out "Happy birthday to you!" louder than anyone else did.

Fred's son, daughter, and his grandchildren were there to wish him a happy ninetieth birthday. It was a day Rosie would always remember. How can a child forget her first birthday party? Although it was a celebration for Fred, he made sure that Rosie was the focus of attention.

The cake was almost as big as Rosie was and had pink roses in each corner. Right in the center, in lacy pink frosting, were the words "Happy Birthday Rosie and Fred." Each guest received a mint alongside a piece of cake and a cup of pink lemonade served on dainty glass plates.

For many days after, the residents talked about the special party. Birthday celebrations were not something new at the Manor, but a party where their Rosie was the center of attention made it special for everyone. They had loved to see her eyes light up with childhood pleasure. Birthdays had become a day to dread, or simply another day of the year for most of them. It was nice to have a reason to enjoy such an occasion.

The following July, Rosie began talking about her upcoming birthday. She looked forward to being eight years old and supposed that Fred would be excited about turning ninety-one.

"When will the party be?" she asked as they walked together.

"Oh, Rosie, there won't be a party this year."

"Why?"

"When you get old, people only celebrate the big ones."

"What are the big ones?" Rosie hadn't lived long enough to think of a birthday as just another day of the year.

"Well, you know—the ones that end in zero or five, like eighty-five, ninety, ninety-five."

"You have to wait five years to have a party?" Rosie's surprised tone said more than her words.

Fred laughed. Her childlike wonder pleased him. "I'm afraid so, my girl."

Rosie didn't talk to him about birthdays again until their birthday arrived. At dinner, Rosie's mother surprised her with a birthday cake in the shape of Winnie the Pooh. It looked so much like her favorite character that Rosie hated to cut into it, but since it was the only dessert for the day, she cut a piece for each resident.

She wanted everyone to wish Fred a happy birthday but he didn't come to dinner. Rosie put his piece of cake on a paper plate and took it down the hall to his room. When she found the door closed she knocked, but Fred did not answer. She returned the cake to the kitchen, supposing Fred was with his children.

That evening just before bedtime, she walked on the quiet sidewalks to the front of the Manor. As she turned the corner to walk along the patio, she saw Fred standing inside the window of the great room. She smiled and waved at him but he didn't seem to notice her.

Rosie tugged open the heavy front door and walked

to Fred's side. She took his hand in hers before he seemed to realize she was there.

"Hi, Rosie." His voice was very quiet.

"Why are you standing here, Fred?"

"I'm just waiting."

"Waiting for what, Fred?" Rosie looked out the window but could not see anyone coming along the walk.

"My family."

"Are they coming tonight?"

"I'm afraid not, Rosie." He took a couple of steps back and sat in his wheelchair.

"Then why are you waiting?" Something didn't make sense.

"Happy birthday, Rosie." Fred's lips curved into a half-smile.

"Happy birthday, Fred. What's it like to be ninety-one?"

"I'm afraid it's lonely. Did you have a good birthday?" Fred wiped his hands across his eyes. He was so tired.

"I saved you a piece of cake. Mama made it for you, too. Do you want it now?" Rosie stepped behind the wheelchair.

"Well, the day's almost over and nobody came. I don't suppose they'll come now. I'd like that cake. Will you push me? I'm too tired to go alone."

Rosie was already pushing him out of the great room into the hall. "Fred, did you eat dinner?"

"No. I was waiting. I guess one's ninety-first birthday isn't a very important day."

"Oh, I don't know. Bessie says that each day is worth celebrating because it's the only one you've got."

"It's good you're learning that young. Don't you forget it." Fred reached over his shoulder and patted her hand.

Rosie pushed his chair into the dining room and up to a table. "You wait right here. I'll get your cake."

It wasn't long before Rosie returned with a ham sandwich, a glass of milk, and a piece of cake with one candle. "Ninety-one candles wouldn't fit. We'll just celebrate the one."

Fred looked at Rosie and smiled, then began to laugh. "I'm sure happy we share a birthday, but from now on I'll celebrate the years since we met. Next year I'll celebrate two instead of ninety-two."

Rosie liked watching Fred eat the sandwich she had

made. He was hungry and he acted as if he enjoyed every bite.

When he was finished, Rosie handed him a small package of matches. "Mama doesn't like me to use matches."

He lit the lone candle. "Make a wish, Rosie," he said, then he blew just hard enough to extinguish the flame.

As the smoke gently curled up into the evening light, she thought of the wish she had made for herself at dinner. She couldn't help but remember the wonderful party of the year before and so her wish had been for another party. Now that wish took on a new meaning. It included someone besides just herself.

"My wish . . . my wish is to share another birthday party with you."

Chapter Eight

THE GARDEN

❧

Residents at Pleasant Manor looked forward to Groundhog Day with a wishful interest. Winter, with its slick walks and penetrating cold, forced them to stay inside for their own safety, so the promise of spring was a welcome reprieve.

Rosie got off the bus after school on February second, and ran down the hall and into the great room. She had seen the poster advertising a special community program to celebrate spring, so she was not surprised at the large crowd of strangers. A woman was speaking into the microphone and those in the group were listening intently.

She walked slowly, trying to see a friend between the long rows of chairs. Then Bessie beckoned to her from the sofa and slid over far enough to allow Rosie to slip in beside her.

"Does anyone recognize this little beauty?" The woman at the microphone held up a small plant with shiny, dark green leaves and a white flower.

"That's a helleborus plant," a man in the back of the room called out.

"Very good," the woman said. "Who can tell me something about this plant?"

Again the man called out. "Its roots are poisonous."

"What else do you know about it?" This time the woman directed her question to the man.

"Well, it starts blooming in the late fall and may bloom through the winter. Sometimes you can even see it blooming through light accumulations of snow."

Bessie turned and cast a questioning look at Rosie. She had never heard of such a thing. Blossoms through the snow? It seemed impossible.

"Anything else?" the woman asked.

The man shook his head.

"Thank you for answering so many of my questions." She turned her attention back to the entire group. "This beautiful little plant is known as a Christmas Rose, not only because it blooms at Christmastime, but also because of an old legend. Following the birth of the Christ child, a poor, young girl named Madelon wanted to worship the newborn King. Longing for a gift to give the special child, she searched the countryside, but it was winter and there was nothing of beauty on the barren ground. She started to cry. Upon seeing her tears, an angel smote the ground, causing a bush with a beautiful white flower to spring forth. It was a fitting gift for the precious Babe."

"Is that true, Bessie?" Rosie leaned into Bessie's side so she could whisper in her ear.

"I don't know. That's quite a story, isn't it?"

"I like it. I hope it's true."

Bessie nodded in agreement. "I like that plant. I'd really like to know if it blooms in . . ." Bessie stopped talking when she saw the lady seated next to them put her finger to her lips.

Winter seemed to be fighting with spring for control of the weather that year. It refused to fade quietly and allow the sunshine to warm the earth. Perhaps the long winter was the reason that Bessie asked the director of Pleasant Manor for a small plot of ground in which to plant some flowers.

"I'm just hankering to get my fingers in the dirt," she said to Rosie as March passed into April.

"May I help?"

"Of course! I couldn't do it without you. I'll get the flowers ordered and as soon as they come we'll start our garden."

The next week, when Rosie ran into Bessie's room she was delighted to find a flat of shiny, dark green plants. "Christmas Roses!" she cried.

"I can't wait to see if these really bloom in the winter. It seems impossible but we're going to find out," Bessie said as she handed Rosie a small box of garden tools.

Outside, Bessie carefully knelt down on the grass that surrounded the tiny plot. She picked up a handful of dirt and let it slip through her fingers. Then she dug a small hole with her trowel and instructed Rosie to pour in some water.

"Now this is how you get the plant out," Bessie said as she loosened one of the plants. "Here, you put it in the hole," she directed. "That's the way, nice and straight. Now press the dirt around it."

Together they worked, making sure to set each plant

firmly in the moist soil before packing dirt around the base. They spaced the plants to fill their garden spot and to give each plant enough room to grow.

"We're done," Rosie said as she covered the roots of the last plant. She jumped to her feet and then reached out her hand to help Bessie.

Bessie took Rosie's hand and tried to push herself up with her other hand. She leaned forward and rocked back and forth to get the momentum to boost herself to a standing position. Suddenly, as her body went forward, she lost her balance and toppled over on her side.

"Bessie!" Rosie cried out.

Bessie shifted to get her legs out from underneath herself and move her body to a sitting position. Each movement was slow and strenuous, causing her to gasp for breath.

"I'll go get help," Rosie said as she ran toward the door of the Manor.

"Rosie . . . wait," Bessie called in a soft, breathless tone.

"But you need help." Rosie turned around and walked back toward the garden.

Bessie stared at her, both eyes wide with surprise.

"I'm okay," she whispered as she lifted up her arm and wiped the sweat off her face with the sleeve of her shirt.

Rosie dropped down beside her and waited until Bessie's raspy, shallow breathing calmed. Then Bessie leaned back on her arms and closed her eyes.

"Bessie, please . . . let me get help."

Bessie just shook her head. "I . . . I don't want . . ." She paused to catch her breath before she could go on. "I don't want somebody telling me I shouldn't be doing this . . ."

It wasn't long before the sound of Bessie's breathing was lost amidst the chatter of birds in the nearby trees. Rosie sat quietly by her side, wishing she could go for help but unwilling to disobey.

When Bessie finally opened her eyes, she stared at the garden and a slow smile flitted over her face. She drew in one deep breath as she turned to Rosie. "Isn't it amazing?"

Rosie started to nod in agreement, and then realized she had no idea what Bessie was talking about. "Amazing? What, Bessie?" she asked.

"Our little garden. Just look at it, Rosie."

Rosie looked across the tiny patch of thin, green

stems. There were many dark leaves but no flowers to mark it as something special.

Bessie leaned over and rested her hand on Rosie's arm. "Rosie, look how straight the rows are. Each plant is set firmly in the rich soil. See how they reach upward. It's going to be a beautiful garden."

When Bessie finally felt as though she could get up, she instructed Rosie to get one of the garden chairs. With Rosie sitting in the chair, Bessie was able to hold onto it and pull herself to her knees. Then she stood up.

Slowly they walked toward the Manor. When they reached the door, Bessie turned for one last look at their little plot of earth. "It feels so good to have a job well done."

During the following weeks, Rosie learned that putting the plants in the ground was only the beginning of their job. Bessie taught her how to tell if the plants needed a little extra water, and then instructed her in how to dig small ditches around each plant to hold the moisture, allowing it to soak into the roots.

"Please let me do that," Rosie pleaded when Bessie started to kneel down to pluck the first weeds. Bessie agreed as she taught her how to remove the roots of the weeds as well as the visible greenery.

Each day they walked together through the halls of the Manor and out into the sunshine to check on their garden. When they completed their tasks, or on those days when nothing needed to be done, they sat on the garden chairs and basked in the sunshine or listened to the whisper of the wind as it dove into their sheltered spot.

Often, when Mama had completed her work in the kitchen, she found them there. "Bessie is a good teacher, Rosie. Your plants look so healthy," she commended them both as she slipped into a garden chair beside them. Sometimes she would even sit and watch as the sun dipped from the sky, leaving a flash of brilliant color. During one of those evenings, she took a deep breath, smiled, and then said quietly to herself, "That is a perfect benediction for the day."

Chapter Nine
ALONE

One day toward the end of Rosie's third grade year, she arrived home from school to find a big change at the Manor. Helen's chair and table were stacked high with boxes outside of her room. Bessie was pacing back and forth in front of them.

"Bessie, what's happening?" Rosie took hold of her arm to stop her.

"Oh, Rosie, you'll never believe it. Helen's husband is coming to live at the Manor so they're moving her in with him." Bessie resumed her pacing without ever totally stopping.

"Her husband?" Rosie shook her head as she thought of the man. "Does Helen want to move?"

"I'm sure they didn't ask her." Bessie was indignant. "Of course she wouldn't understand anyway."

Just then Helen walked out of her room and up the

hall. She paid no attention to her personal belongings packed in boxes outside the room.

Two aides picked up the boxes and put them on a cart. Then, in a matter of minutes, Helen's things were gone from the place where she had lived for many years. Bessie stood in the middle of the hall glaring at the workers, who paid no attention to her. They were just following instructions. She had no say in the matter.

"Bessie," the nurse said as she took hold of Bessie's arm and guided her into the room. "We need your help. I know this is hard for you to lose your roommate, but she needs to be with her husband. Now you know Helen is confused and will keep coming to this room. Please tell her she doesn't live here anymore and call one of us. It will take a while before Helen remembers she has a new room."

"What if she doesn't like the change?" Bessie was more concerned about Helen than about herself.

"There's no reason she won't like it. Her husband wants to be able to keep an eye on her."

"Really? He could have been doing that for years now." Bessie always got upset when people talked about

Helen's husband. As far as she could see, his monthly visits didn't show much concern.

"Will you help us, Bessie? You know our hands are tied—he pays the bill." The nurse waited at the door for an answer.

"Helen will always be welcome in my room, but if she's happy with her husband, I'll try to help her find her way."

"Thanks, Bessie. I've got to get his room ready. He'll be here soon."

Rosie was watching by the front door when Helen's husband arrived. He hobbled through the door with a cane in each hand. "Where's my room?" he asked the aide who was carrying his suitcase.

"Down the hall to your right, sir."

"Has Helen moved in?" His voice was gruff. He was not one for conversation.

"Yes, sir. Her things are there."

Rosie walked down the hall behind them, leaving enough distance so they would not know she was watching them. As they reached the corner, Helen walked around it and nearly smacked into her husband.

"Watch where you're . . ." he blurted out before he

realized who it was. "Oh, Helen . . . ," he said to her, but she didn't even notice.

Running into him brought only a slight interruption in her walk. She continued on her way without recognizing him.

The days that followed were very difficult for Bessie and Helen. Each time Helen was ready to lie down she went to Bessie's room. If Bessie was gone Helen went inside, then walked in circles around and around the room like a caged animal until someone found her. She was usually so upset by then that her high-pitched squeal resounded through the halls as she resisted everyone's demands. Her mind was locked into a pattern, and no matter what anybody said she was sure she belonged in that room.

Rosie finally found a way to get Helen to go to her new room without a great fight. During one of Helen's troubling episodes, Rosie ran to Helen's new room and grabbed the quilt off her bed. Helen's mother had made the quilt—it was one of the few possessions Helen recognized as her own. When Helen saw it, she quieted down. Then she followed Rosie as she carried the quilt to her new room. Only after Rosie spread it across her bed would she lie down.

She took no notice of her husband, perhaps because the aide always pulled the curtain to divide the room. Helen's husband didn't seem to mind. In fact, it probably gave him the privacy he wanted.

"When will you get a new roommate?" Rosie asked Bessie as they sat on the front porch and watched the stars flicker in the sky.

"Soon, I'm sure."

"The dog! There's a dog in my room!" Helen screamed as she pushed her way past the aide who tried to block the front door.

"Helen, there's no dog." The aide's voice was sharp as she reached for Helen's arm.

Helen pushed her aside and headed across the porch. She was agitated.

"Helen!" the aide yelled. "Helen, get back in here!"

"Rosie, we'd better help her." Bessie got to her feet as Rosie raced to Helen's side.

"Helen, I'll get the dog," Rosie said.

Without a word, Helen turned and followed Rosie through the door. She didn't even pause at her new room. Rosie ran ahead of her to Bessie's room, did her usual check, and met Helen at the door.

"The dog's gone," she said as she gently guided Helen past the room. Helen walked off without another word.

It took Helen three weeks to realize that her home was in a different place. During that time, her fearful cry about the dog echoed through the halls many times each day. Then one day everything changed. Helen walked back from breakfast and turned right into her new room as though that was where she had always been. She never went to her old room again nor did she cry out about the dog. In fact, she did not say another word until the day of the dance.

Dances were a weekly event at the Manor. Although few of the residents could stand and dance with a partner, all of them enjoyed being pushed in their wheelchairs as the CD player pumped out the music embedded in their memories. The old tunes reminded them of their youth when they had met friends and sweethearts on the dance floor.

Rosie always helped Mama on dance days. She could carry small trays of cookies and punch from the kitchen to the great room so her mama didn't have to make so many trips. After the refreshments were prepared, Rosie helped push the residents onto the dance floor. She had seen Helen and her husband enter the great room. He had his hand on her elbow and guided her to two chairs in the corner. Throughout the dance, they sat alone, just watching. Rosie had been surprised as she walked by them to see that Helen's husband was smiling. She had never seen him smile. Helen was sitting upright, her face showing no expression. It seemed that even the music was not getting through to Helen's closed mind.

Then all of a sudden Helen shook her head and stood up. In her haste, she almost knocked over a chair that stood in her way. Her mouth was open wide, her eyes locked in an expression of distress. When she reached the table where Rosie stood, she grabbed Rosie's arm.

"Helen, what's the matter?"

"That man!"

Rosie waited for her to say more but Helen just stood there pointing to her husband and shaking her head.

"What about him, Helen?" Rosie asked.

Her words came out in a shriek of panic. "That man was holding my hand."

The nurse had stepped to Helen's side in time to hear her explanation. "Helen, it's all right. He's your husband."

Helen looked at the nurse for a moment and shook her head. Then in a loud, clear voice she cried, "My husband? I don't have a husband!"

The moment passed as quickly as it had begun. Helen's face, that had been so full of expression, turned back to a blank stare. She turned and walked from the room.

Helen's husband stood and left without speaking to anyone. He never attended another dance. In fact, he stayed in his room most of the time. The only time Rosie saw him was during mealtimes, when he and Helen sat at their own table and ate. When he finished he walked out by himself and shuffled down the hall to his room.

"I worry about him," Bessie said to Rosie one day after he passed by them without speaking.

"Why? Is he sick?" Rosie asked.

"No, he's so alone." Bessie shook her head as she watched him walk down the hall.

"There's lots of people here, Bessie." Rosie held out her hands as though wondering why Bessie could not see them.

Bessie's laughter lasted only a moment. She could never resist Rosie's innocence. Then in her quiet, serious voice she explained, "Oh, Rosie, some people are all alone when they're surrounded by people. Just look at him. He is alone. He never reaches out to another person."

Chapter Ten
INA

If Rosie had been like many other children her age, she would have slept late on the first day of summer vacation. But it was not long after she heard the door close quietly behind her mother that she got up and dressed. After she had made her bed and washed the nighttime dishes, she ran out the door and skipped over to the Manor.

She saw some new faces at the desk. During the summer months, many of the regular staff had time off and students came in to take their places. Since it was still early, most of the residents were in their rooms preparing for the day. Although she was going to the kitchen to help Mama, she turned quickly into Bessie's room to tell her good morning.

To her surprise, Rosie found herself face to face with someone she had never seen. In fact, she had never seen anyone who looked anything like that someone who stood in Bessie's room. She could tell it was a woman by the two gray streaked braids wrapped around her head, but her features were so grossly distorted that she would have thought her a man. The woman wore dark glasses that failed to hide her puffy, purple-red cheeks. There was only a small lump where her nose should have been. Jagged lines covered her forehead and cheeks. From her neck protruded sagging skin that swayed back and forth with any movement.

"I . . . I . . . I'm s-s-sorry," Rosie stuttered as she backed away from the woman whose looks horrified her.

"Good morning." The woman held out her hand.

Rosie looked past her, searching for Bessie, until she heard water running in the bathroom and realized she was alone with the woman. Without thinking, she backed out through the open door.

"Are you by chance Bessie's friend?" The woman did not seem to notice Rosie had left the room.

When Rosie heard Bessie's name a bit of the fear that swarmed in her mind lifted and she could respond. "Yes, I'm Rosie."

"Ah, Rosie—what a lovely name."

The woman's smile forced the purple-red skin to melt into a mass of wrinkles. She looked like a head of red cabbage with sunglasses. Rosie began to giggle as she thought of the comparison.

"Come here, my child. May I touch your face?" The woman lifted both hands into the air as though she was reaching for something nearby, but she did not take a step.

It was a strange request. Rosie hesitated. She did not want the stranger to touch her.

"I won't hurt you, Rosie." The woman's voice did not match her looks. It was soft and musical, with an accent Rosie could hear but not identify.

Rosie stepped forward slowly and touched the woman's hands. The woman laid them on Rosie's shoulders and then on the top of her head before stroking down her pigtails. "Lovely hair. It's so thick and soft. What color is it?"

"Brown," Rosie spoke without thinking.

The woman's hands were on Rosie's cheeks and then her chin. "Do you have lovely dark brown eyes to match?"

Rosie stared at the woman, her mind racing as she finally understood what was happening. "You . . . you're blind," Rosie whispered.

"Yes, I am. Thank you for letting me feel what you look like."

"Rosie, you're up and at it early." Bessie opened the bathroom door and walked toward her. "You've met Ina?"

Rosie nodded her head in answer. Her throat felt so tight she was afraid to speak.

"She's my new roommate. I told her you'd be coming by." Bessie hung her robe in the closet as she talked. "Would you like to help us? We're going to put Ina's things away so she can find them."

Rosie didn't answer.

Bessie turned and looked at Rosie, aware that something was bothering her. It wasn't until she put her arm around Rosie's shoulders and found her trembling that she realized what had happened. "Ina, Rosie and I are going to walk up to the kitchen to say hello to her mother. We'll help you with your clothes in just a few minutes."

Rosie was grateful for the chance to get away from

the stranger. She needed time to think, to talk to Bessie about the woman. Bessie kept her arm around Rosie's shoulders as they walked down the hall, but she didn't say anything. She knew Rosie would confide in her when she was ready.

They were almost to the kitchen before Rosie broke the silence. "That lady scared me."

"She scared you?" Bessie stopped and looked intently at Rosie.

"She just looks so, so. . . . Oh, Bessie, she looks like a monster."

"She startled you, didn't she? I would have told you she was coming if I had known." Bessie sat down on the edge of the old sofa and patted the seat next to her.

Rosie sat down and leaned against Bessie. "What's the matter with her? Why does she look like that?"

"Ina was hurt in a fire. It nearly killed her. From what I've heard it's a miracle she lived. Her parents finally brought her to America for medical help when she was a teenager."

"Did you know her then?"

"Ina lived about forty miles away from where I was raised. I knew of the accident, but I didn't see her until about twenty years ago when I needed help after Henry died. Ina came and stayed with me for company until I could get by on my own. I remember being shocked about the way she looked then, but now I hardly notice."

"But, Bessie, how can you stand to look at her?"

Bessie's forehead wrinkled as it always did when she was thinking. It took her several minutes before she finally took Rosie's hand and looked straight into her face. "Rosie, I guess I don't see Ina's ugly scars because inside she's so beautiful."

"What do you mean?"

Bessie paused again. She was searching for a way to teach her young friend about real beauty. "Rosie, who is the most beautiful person in the world to you?"

Without hesitating Rosie said, "You are, Bessie."

Bessie was taken aback. When she asked the question, she had not even considered Rosie would name her. "Me? Why, you dear child."

She gathered Rosie up in a tight hug. It wasn't until Rosie felt a teardrop on her face that she moved from the warm circle of Bessie's arms.

"Don't mind these tears, dear. You just made me

very happy. Now look at me. I have old wrinkled skin that is dotted with age spots. Why do you think I'm beautiful?"

"Because you are my best friend and you are kind to everyone."

"My girl, you already know about beauty. Ina's one of the most beautiful people I have ever known. Look beyond her skin and you will see her lovely soul."

"You mean she's beautiful like you?"

Bessie laughed. It had been years since she thought of herself as beautiful. "Maybe beautiful like you, my child. Nobody has told me I was beautiful since my Henry died twenty years ago. I can't wait to see him again so I can tell him all about you."

Rosie jerked her head around in surprise. "Isn't Henry dead?"

"Of course he's dead."

"Then how will you tell him about me?" Rosie leaned closer to Bessie, waiting for another laugh to dismiss her words as a joke.

There was no laugh. When Bessie replied, her voice was hushed but sure. "Rosie, dear, Henry's body is dead but his spirit is very much alive."

"It is?" Rosie's eyes and mouth were open wide. She did not try to hide the surprise from her face.

Bessie nodded her head, then bit her bottom lip to stop it from shaking. "Oh, yes. Someday I'll be with—"

"Rosie, there you are. Can you come help me with the juice?" Mama called from the kitchen door.

Bessie patted her hand as she stood to leave. "We'll help Ina later."

"Later" came that afternoon. At Ina's direction, Bessie and Rosie lined the shelves with her belongings. They placed each item carefully so Ina could find it in just the right spot.

When the task was complete Bessie said, "Hold your arm like this, Rosie." Bessie bent her arm and held it out for Ina to grasp.

Rosie held out her arm for Ina's other hand. With Ina between them, they could walk anywhere. They were Ina's guides as they kept her safe and taught her about her new surroundings. It was the first of their daily walks around the Manor.

On one of those walks, several weeks into the summer, Rosie heard a little boy whisper to his mother. He was trying to be quiet, so she barely heard him until the word "monster" darted straight at her. As Rosie jerked her head around to look at the boy, she saw a look of fear plastered on his face. His eyes were on Ina.

Rosie knew that word. Had she not felt the same? As they passed by the boy and his mother, Rosie looked at Ina, really looked at her. It was clear that her face had not healed—the scars, the color, the sagging skin were still there, but they did not bother Rosie anymore. Without thinking, she patted Ina's hand in the crook of her arm. It was then that she realized that to her, Ina was almost as beautiful as Bessie.

Chapter Eleven

HALLOWEEN

❧⟡❧

Fourth grade settled into a routine of bus rides, schoolwork, and weekends. The bus driver didn't question Rosie again; he just stopped and let her off without speaking. She liked it that way. Once she left the Manor, her shyness took over and made her uncomfortable talking to anyone.

When October rolled around Rosie began making plans for the Halloween celebration. She knew there would never be a Halloween holiday to match the Haunt that Bessie and Helen had planned. Nothing could come close to that special event, but Bessie had always made sure they carved pumpkins and iced orange sugar cookies.

"Bessie, can we carve the pumpkins next week?" Rosie was pointing at the days on the calendar. "There are only three weeks left."

"Well, let's see. Hmm, three weeks. If we keep them outside where it's cooler we should be all right. I'll get them ordered." Bessie picked up the phone and made her annual call. "You'll deliver them to the Manor then? Great—five should do nicely."

The following week when the pumpkins were delivered, Rosie ran to Bessie's room. "Come on, the pumpkins are here."

Bessie was lying on her bed. She pushed herself to the side of the bed but just sat there looking at Rosie. "Rosie, you're big enough to carve those pumpkins without my help. Would you mind if I rested today and Ina helped you?"

Rosie walked to Bessie's bed and felt her head as she had seen the nurses do. "Are you sick?"

"I'm not feeling quite like I'd like to." Bessie lay back on the bed and pulled her blanket up around her neck.

"Bessie hasn't been feeling well for the last three days. I was hoping the doctor would come and see her today," Ina said as she reached over and took Rosie's arm. "I'd love to help with those pumpkins."

Rosie hesitated for a minute, looking from Bessie to

Ina. It wouldn't be the same without Bessie to give her ideas about where to stick the knife for the best-looking face. Could Ina be of help when she couldn't see?

"Where do we do the carving?" Ina was gently pushing Rosie's arm, encouraging her to leave the room.

They covered a table in the craft shop with newspaper and got one sharp knife. "Now, Rosie, you'll have to tell me how Bessie helped you."

"Well, she pointed to the pumpkin and told me where to put the eyes and nose. Then she made a face and I'd copy it with my knife."

Ina laughed. "That Bessie sure does know how to do things right. How's this?" She opened her mouth as wide as it would go into a big round circle. "Don't you think a pumpkin would look fine with a mouth like that to shine a candle through?"

Rosie almost laughed when she looked at Ina's open mouth surrounded by the purple-red wrinkles. Ina was trying so hard to help her. "That's great, Ina," she said as she stabbed the knife into the pumpkin and began carving a large round circle.

As Rosie carved one pumpkin, Ina felt the next one with her rough, scarred hands. She could point out the flaws and give suggestions that a person with sight would never consider.

"Well, what do you think, Rosie? Do we have some scary pumpkins?" Ina asked as Rosie put the top on the last carved pumpkin.

Rosie looked over the table and decided that she had never seen pumpkins quite like those. They were indeed the spookiest pumpkins she had ever seen. "I wish you could see them. They are scarrrrry."

"Show me the best one." Ina held out her hands for Rosie to direct. Then she felt along the cuts that marked the eyes, nose, and mouth. "You're a real pumpkin artist, Rosie."

When Bessie woke up that afternoon, she found the very best pumpkin sitting on the table beside her bed. She looked at it a moment, then shook her head and smiled as she said to herself, "Ina will do."

"Did you call me, Bessie?" Ina was sitting in the corner of the room waiting for her friend to wake up.

"No, Ina. The pumpkin is just right. Did Rosie have a good time carving it?"

"I hope so, because I did. Are you feeling better?"

"I'm just so tired. I think I'll sleep again for a

while." Bessie was asleep before Ina could ask another question.

Some days Bessie seemed stronger, able to talk and laugh softly when Rosie visited her. On other days, she was very quiet and asked only a few questions about Rosie's day. After school each day, Rosie ran into her friend's room to see if Bessie was ready for one of their walks.

"Maybe tomorrow," Bessie would reply.

The day before Halloween, Rosie ran into Bessie's room and found her sitting in her wheelchair. "Bessie, you're better!" Rosie cried as she ran to hug her.

"Much better," Bessie said, holding Rosie close. "You didn't think I would miss Halloween, did you? Now how about that walk? Can you push me? I'm not quite up to going on my own."

"Oh, yes. Where are we going?" Rosie asked as she pushed Bessie through the door of the room and out into the long hallway.

"To the garden, of course. I can't wait to see how it's grown. And I'd like to see all those pumpkins you and Ina carved."

Rosie pushed her down the hall toward the side exit,

stopping frequently so that Bessie's friends could exclaim over how good she looked or just how nice it was to see her. And of course they had to stop at each nurse's station so Bessie could see the pumpkins.

"You and Ina did such a good . . ." Bessie's voice gave way. She cleared her throat but didn't finish her sentence.

When they came to the side door Rosie propped it open so she could push Bessie outside. As she turned to close the door, Bessie grabbed her hand.

"Oh, Rosie, it's beautiful! I see some white. Is that a rose in the corner?"

Rosie stepped around the garden to the far corner, knelt down, and carefully picked the one blossom from the patch. She held it like a treasure as she carried it to Bessie, delighting over the shiny white petals with pink tips. Rosie presented the flower to Bessie with a courtly bow.

"Thank you, Rosie, for taking such good care of our garden," Bessie said.

Bessie had now seen her garden, and though she wanted to stay and soak in the beauty, her strength was gone. Rosie pushed her back to her room, where the nurse helped her into bed.

The next day after school, Rosie ran to Bessie's room, hoping to take her to the great room for the Halloween program, but Bessie was in bed. "Are you all right?" Rosie asked as she sat in the chair beside the bed.

"I'm fine—just a little tired. Are there more roses?"

"I'll go see," Rosie said as she headed for the door.

After that, Rosie checked the garden, in anticipation of Bessie's question, before she went to her room. For several weeks, she reported that there were no more blossoms. During that time, she often found Bessie sitting in her recliner, sometimes in her wheelchair, but she seldom left her room and never accepted Rosie's offer to take her to their garden.

The week before Thanksgiving, Rosie rushed into Bessie's room to tell her the news. There were three blossoms. "Do you want to go see them?" Rosie's voice was hopeful.

Bessie smiled. "I can't today, but soon, Rosie. Soon."

Chapter Twelve

THE GIFT

That Thanksgiving was truly a day for giving thanks at Pleasant Manor, because Bessie was able to join her friends in the dining room. Although her laughter was quieter than in the past, her warm recognition of each resident set a caring tone for the day.

The next morning Rosie walked with Mama to the Manor. Since Mama didn't need her help until breakfast was prepared, Rosie ran to check on the garden. As she opened the Manor door, the sun broke through the leafless boughs of frost-laden trees and lit up crystals of snow on the ground. Rosie rushed out the door, feeling like she was in an enchanted ice castle.

"Oh!" she exclaimed. For there, totally covering their garden, were bunches of Christmas Roses. Their moist surfaces shimmered with movement as though dancing in the light when the sun bounced off each glistening petal.

Rosie turned from the garden and ran through the halls to Bessie's room. "Bessie, you have to see them. They are amazing!" she cried as she dashed through the door.

"The Christmas Roses?" Bessie asked as she slid her feet into her slippers and sat down in her wheelchair.

"Oh, yes, Bessie. Do you want to go see them?"

Bessie hesitated only a moment before giving Rosie directions. "Please get my coat and a blanket. I wouldn't miss this for the world."

"Where are you two going in such a hurry?" Clarice from the craft shop asked when she met them in the hall.

"To the garden," Rosie and Bessie replied in unison.

"Whoa." Clarice put her hand on the arm of the wheelchair. "I was just coming to give you this, Bessie." She held up a small Christmas sack with tissue paper coming out of the top. "We finally got it done, just like you ordered, and, if I do say so myself, it's beautiful. Let me show it to you," she said as she reached into the sack.

"No, please don't take it out. I'll just take it with me." Bessie held out her hand for the package. "Thanks. I know it will be perfect." She set the sack by her side.

"Well, I guess you can go then. Enjoy the garden," Clarice said as she stepped aside to let them by.

Rosie looked outside as she propped open the door of the Manor. She was grateful the sun had not melted the tiny snowflakes. She could not see Bessie's face as she pushed her through the door but she heard her exclamation of absolute delight. "Oh, Rosie, it *is* amazing! I have never seen anything so beautiful! It . . ." Bessie stopped as tears choked her voice.

Rosie leaned over and put her head on Bessie's shoulder, then draped an arm around her neck. "Bessie, do you believe the legend?"

Bessie nodded her head, then cleared her throat and whispered, "What a perfect gift for Christ."

Rosie knew better than to let Bessie stay in the cold for long, so their time in the Christmas Rose garden was short. But that was all right. After all, it was only the beginning of the season for their Christmas Roses. Surely they would have many days to enjoy the fruits of their labor, Rosie thought as she carefully pushed Bessie through the door of the Manor and back to her room.

The next morning Bessie was too weary to leave her room; the next, she was too weary to leave her bed.

"I'm sorry, Bessie." Rosie's voice quivered as she leaned down beside her. "Oh, why did I take you out . . . ?"

"Nonsense! How would I have seen our roses? I didn't wait all this time for nothing." She reached over and covered Rosie's hand with hers, then closed her eyes as she drew in long, sustained breaths.

After a moment she opened her eyes and then waited until Rosie's eyes met hers. She smiled slightly and whispered, "True living is not about breathing. It's about happiness. You gave me that, Rosie."

Rosie left when Bessie fell asleep. Several times during the day she stopped by and found her still sleeping. Ina, ever watchful of her friend, sat in a chair next to her.

That became a familiar sight to Rosie in the days

that followed. It didn't matter when she stopped by their room—before school, after school, or in the evening when she left the Manor with her mother—Ina was at Bessie's side. In fact, Ina left her friend only to eat or do something with Rosie at Bessie's request.

Rosie had seen residents become ill and stay in bed for weeks or even months before they were well enough to get up and go about their usual activities. Bessie had just been through such a period, but she had rallied.

Until the first week in December, Rosie never considered the possibility that Bessie might not get well. When Rosie ran in after school, Bessie asked her to sit down in the chair by the bed.

Ina moved from her place and stood behind Rosie as Bessie reached out and folded Rosie's hand in her own. "Rosie, my girl," she paused. Just those words seemed to make her tired.

Rosie leaned closer to her bed and could hear the loud, raspy sound of her breathing. Under the cover, Bessie's chest rose high and then dropped with each breath. She tried to speak, but it was so hard that she stopped after a couple of words.

"Bessie, can Rosie come back later? Maybe the nurse can help you sit up so it will be easier to talk." Ina leaned over to smooth Bessie's hair from her face.

Bessie shook her head. "No, I must tell Rosie now." She took a sip of water out of the straw that Ina held close to her mouth. After taking two deep breaths, she began again.

"Rosie, my girl. I'll be leaving Pleasant Manor."

"Leaving? But where will you go?"

Bessie smiled, and Rosie thought she would laugh her old jovial laugh, but Bessie did not have enough energy.

"I'm going home."

"But Bessie, this is home." Rosie grabbed hold of Bessie's wrists.

"Home to Henry. You'll be all right without me now that Ina's here." When Bessie's words finally made sense to Rosie's confused mind she began to cry and put her head next to Bessie's.

Bessie stroked Rosie's long hair. "Now, no more tears. I'm not going today."

When Bessie's arm fell down to the bed, Rosie lifted her head and looked up. Then she felt Ina's hand on her shoulder.

"Come, sit beside me, Rosie. Bessie is asleep."

Ina put her arm around Rosie just as Bessie did when she was sad. "Just think about that reunion she'll have with Henry. Can you just see it all, Rosie?"

It was strange how one minute Rosie felt as though she were going to weep forever. The next, she was laughing as Ina painted a picture of that reunion with her words.

Ina lowered her voice to sound like a man. "'Why, Bessie, what took you so long?' Henry will say. 'I was having too much fun with Rosie to come to heaven,' Bessie will answer. Won't our Bessie make heaven fun? Can't you just see it, Rosie?"

Rosie leaned into Ina's arm, grateful for her warmth and strength. Neither of them moved until the nurse came.

"Dinner is ready in the dining room. You'd better get down there before the food is gone." The nurse turned on the light and raised the head of Bessie's bed.

Bessie opened her eyes and smiled at Rosie before she left the room.

After that, Rosie hated to leave Bessie and go to school for the day. When the bus arrived at the Manor each afternoon, Rosie dashed through the front door and down the hall to make sure Bessie was still there. Her greatest fear was finding the room empty without being able to say good-bye.

On Friday, two weeks before Christmas, Rosie rushed into Bessie's room and found Ina combing through Bessie's long hair. When Bessie heard Rosie's voice, she looked up and smiled. Rosie bent down and wrapped her arms around Bessie's neck as she gently hugged her.

"I love you, Rosie." Bessie's voice was so weak that Rosie could barely hear the words, but she knew them by heart.

"I love you, Bessie," she replied as she took Bessie's hand and sat beside her bed.

The next morning, Rosie and Mama left their little stone house while it was still dark. As they opened the back door to the Manor, they found Ina sitting alone in a chair, just inside the entryway.

"Ina, what are you doing up so early?" Mama asked.

"Just waiting for you."

Ina reached out and felt for Rosie's head, then slid her hands down her arms to touch her hands. "Rosie, Bessie wanted me to tell you there's a wonderful reunion going on right now. She loves you, little lady. You gave her a reason for living."

Rosie buried her head against Mama's shoulder and cried. As the tears fell, she knew she should be laughing, or at least smiling, as she thought about the reunion, but she couldn't stop the tears. An awful loneliness tugged at her heart.

Mama pulled her close, wanting to comfort her though overwhelmed with her own feelings of loss. She reflected on Bessie's countless acts of tender, loving influence toward her daughter and the impact they had on her own life. Together they mourned, seemingly lost in grief until Ina touched Rosie's shoulder.

"Rosie, this is for you," Ina said as she handed her a brightly colored Christmas sack with tissue paper coming out of the top.

Rosie turned in Mama's arms. "What is it?" she asked as she wiped the tears from her cheeks.

"A gift from Bessie."

"Bessie?" The name burst from her lips in a strained whisper.

Ina nodded. "It's your Christmas present. I think Bessie would like you to have it now. Merry Christmas, Rosie."

Rosie took the sack, reached inside, and felt something sharp. She pulled it out and gasped with delight. For there, in a beautifully framed, ornate metal casing, was a watercolor painting of a Christmas Rose with silvery drops of moisture glistening from the shiny white petals.

"It . . . it looks just like our roses," Rosie said quietly as she stared at the picture. "It's so . . . so amazing. Oh, I love it. I wish I could thank Bessie."

"Look in the sack. There's a card," Ina said.

Rosie pulled out the small, single page. "Shall I read it out loud?"

"Please," Ina said softly as Rosie began to read.

Christmas Rose

As sparks of light through winter snows,
You touched my heart like a Christmas Rose.

My days were dark with deep despair.
All hope had flown until you were there.
Then through your gentle, loving way
You cast your light on my wintry day,
And turned me from my bed of woes,
My hope, my joy, my Christmas Rose.

Rosie started to read the poem aloud for the second time, then stopped and read it quietly to herself. When she finished she looked at Ina, her eyes bright with tears. "Does that mean me, Ina? Am I a Christmas Rose?"

"Indeed you are. Why even your name . . ." Ina stopped. Bessie's poem had said it all.

Rosie turned back into the comfort of her mama's arms.

"Bessie loved you so much," Mama whispered.

Rosie nodded. She knew that. Bessie had told her so many times. She could still hear those words as Bessie whispered them.

Then from distant moments together came the thought—*Some people are alone when they are surrounded by people* . . . Bessie's voice spoke the words clearly to Rosie's mind. She wanted to hold on to them—words were all she had left of the woman who had loved her, the woman who had taught her so much about living. Words seemed like such a fragile tie, and yet they were there in her mind, as fresh and sure as the moment Bessie had said them. *They're alone because they don't reach out to another person.*

Rosie turned from Mama, realizing that Ina was still standing next to them, alone. She put her arms around Ina's waist and hugged her with all her might. They stood together, arms wrapped tightly around each other. Rosie knew she was not alone.

About the Author

Robyn Buttars has been fortunate to live in the beautiful Cache Valley of northern Utah. She and her husband, Kent, are the parents of six children. They have one special daughter-in-law and a grandson. Professionally, she is a registered nurse with experience in pediatrics and geriatrics. Along with writing, Robyn enjoys composing, traveling, and reading.

You can visit the author at www.robynbuttars.com